nickelodeon

PAW PATROL

Awesome Sticker Collection

A GOLDEN BOOK • NEW YORK

© 2017 Spin Master PAW Productions Inc. All rights reserved. Published in the United States by Golden Books, an imprint of Random House Children's Books, a division of Penguin Random House LLC, 1745 Broadway, New York, NY 10019, and in Canada by Penguin Random House Canada Limited, Toronto. Golden Books, A Golden Book, and the G colophon are registered trademarks of Penguin Random House LLC. PAW Patrol and all related titles, logos, and characters are trademarks of Spin Master Ltd. Nickelodeon and all related titles and logos are trademarks of Viacom International Inc. ISBN 978-1-5247-1682-0
randomhousekids.com
MANUFACTURED IN CHINA
10 9 8 7 6 5

Use the key to color this picture.

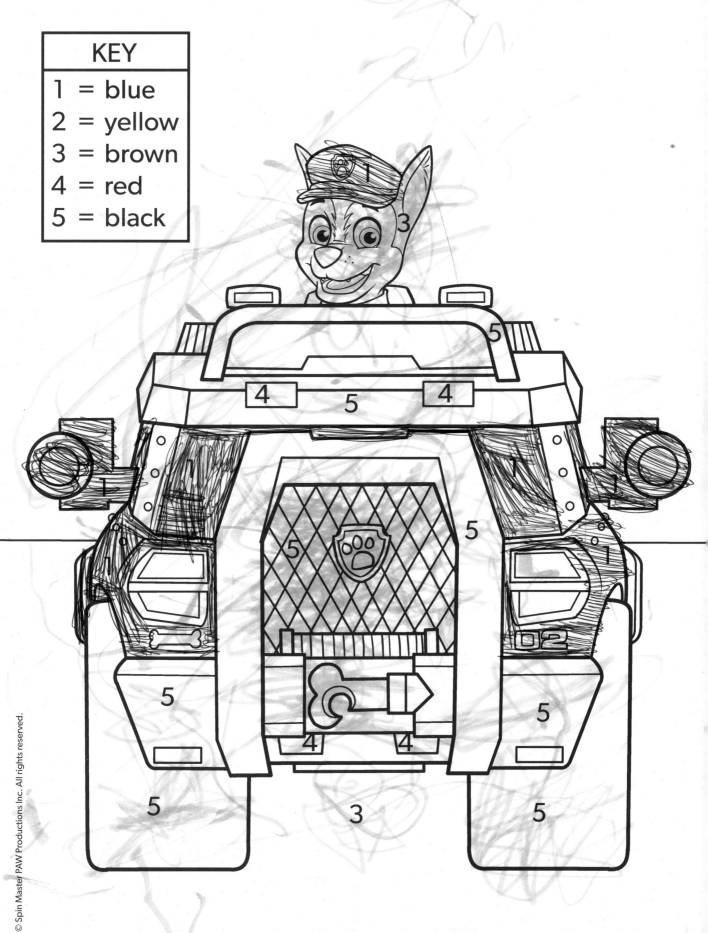

KEY
1 = blue
2 = yellow
3 = brown
4 = red
5 = black

ROCKY

ALL PAWS ON DECK!

ZUMA

MARSHALL

CHASE

Circle the Marshall who is different.

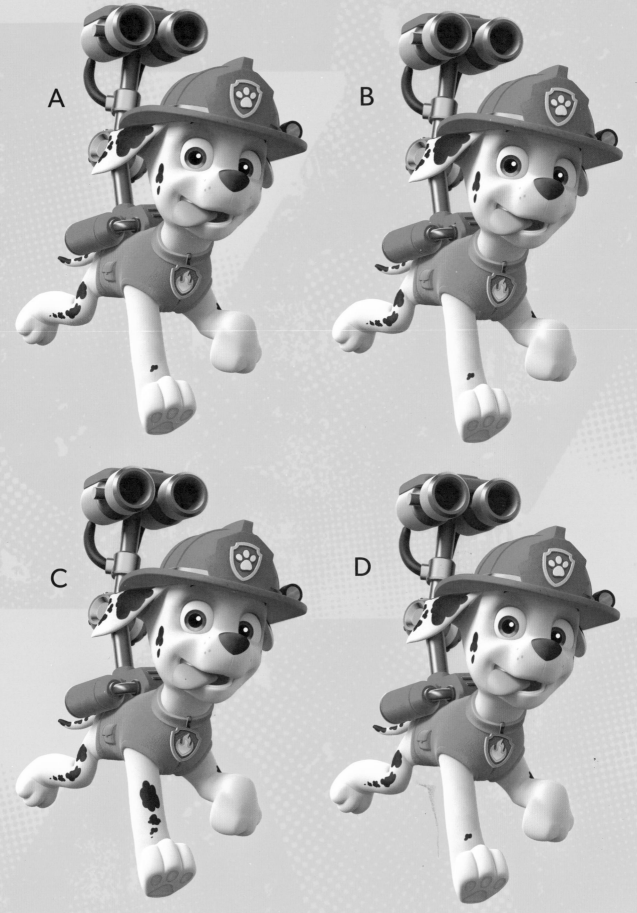

ANSWER: C.

RUBBLE

Help Rubble get to his Digger.

START

FINISH

Don't lose it—reuse it!
Place a recycling sticker
on Rocky's pail.

ZUMA

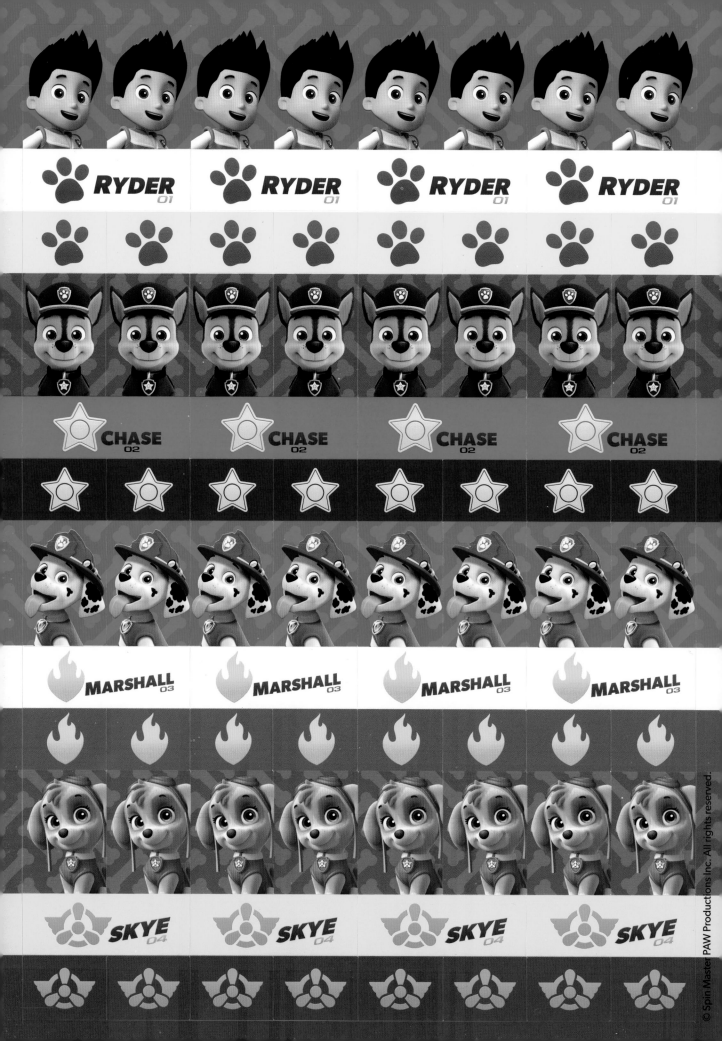

RYDER
01

CHASE
02

MARSHALL
03

SKYE
04

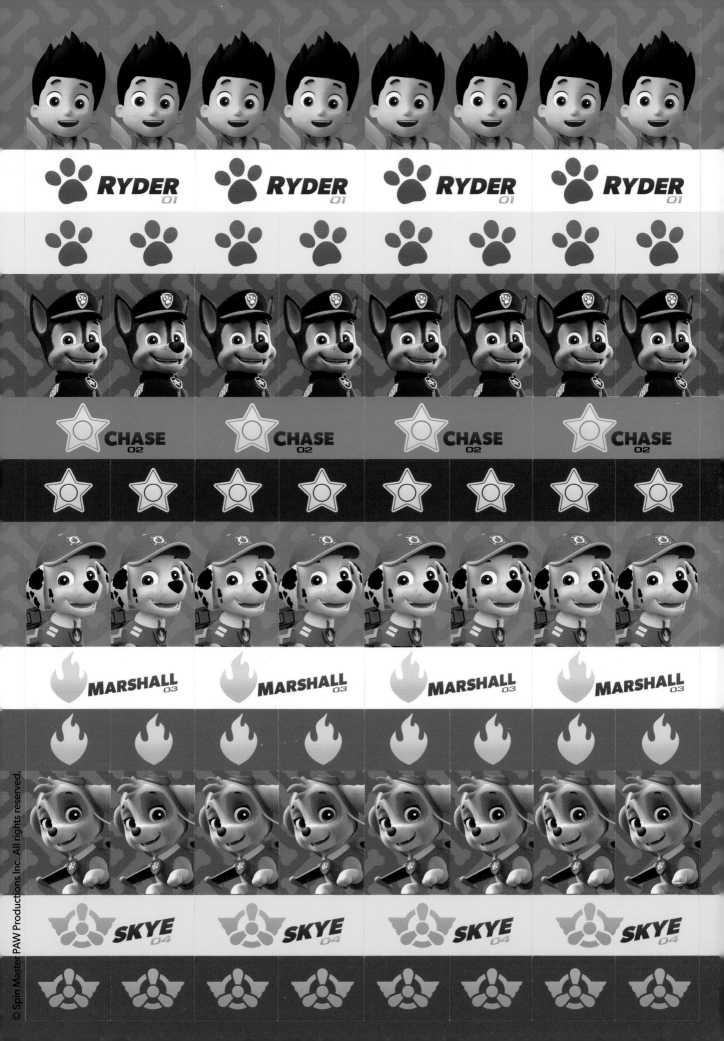

RYDER
01

CHASE
02

MARSHALL
03

SKYE
04

Help Zuma get to his hovercraft.

START

FINISH

Match each member of the team to his or her vehicle.

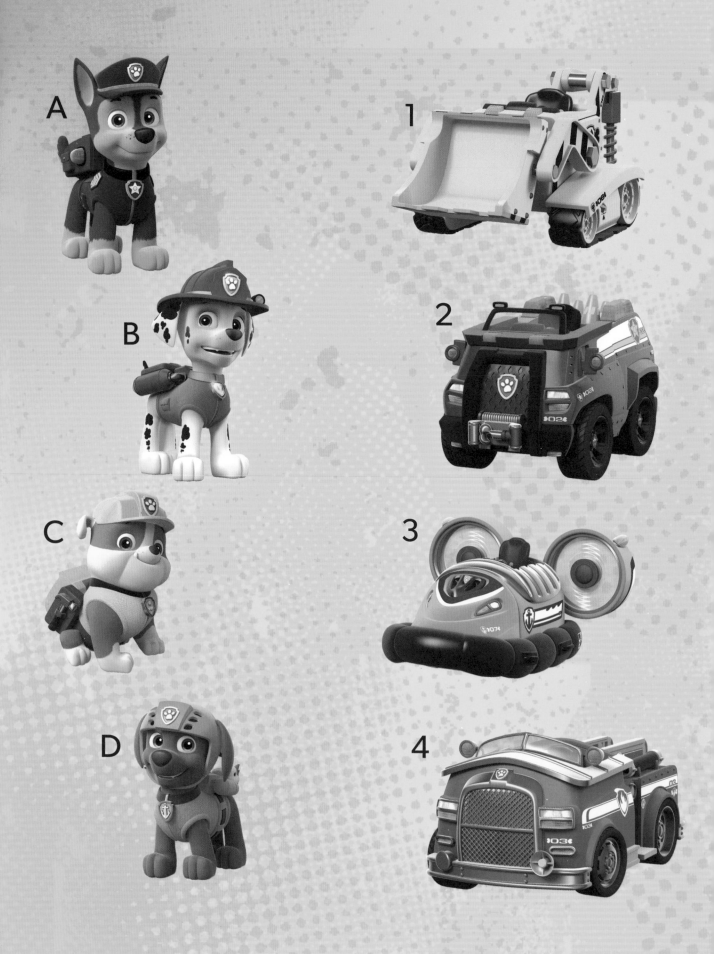

A

1

B

2

C

3

D

4

E

F

G

5

6

7

ANSWER: A-2, B-4, C-1, D-3, E-6, F-5, and G-7.

Can you help Ryder find these pups in the puzzle?

CHASE • SKYE • MARSHALL • ROCKY
RUBBLE • ZUMA • EVEREST • TRACKER

```
G X O V Q M T R J Z
Z U M A E A F Q D M
V E U G M R T D E J
C H A S E S R R V Z
E V W X A H A U E T
Q L E G C A C B R G
R O C K Y L K B E F
K K A B E L E L S E
S K Y E U S R E T M
I W E X M R T P U A
```

ANSWER:

PAW Patrol to the Lookout!
Use your stickers to complete the scene.

ROBO DOG

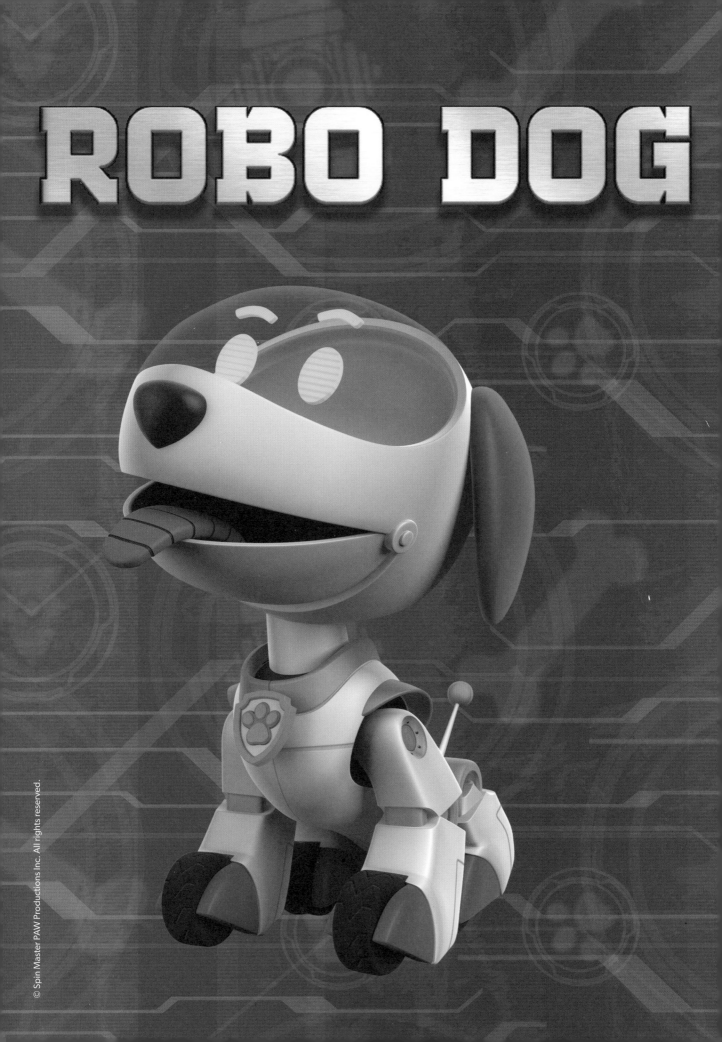

Pup Treats!
(A game for two players)

Take turns with a friend connecting two dots with a straight line. When the line you draw completes a square, put your initials in the square and give yourself two points. If the square has a bone in it, give yourself two extra points. When all the boxes have been made, whoever has more points wins!

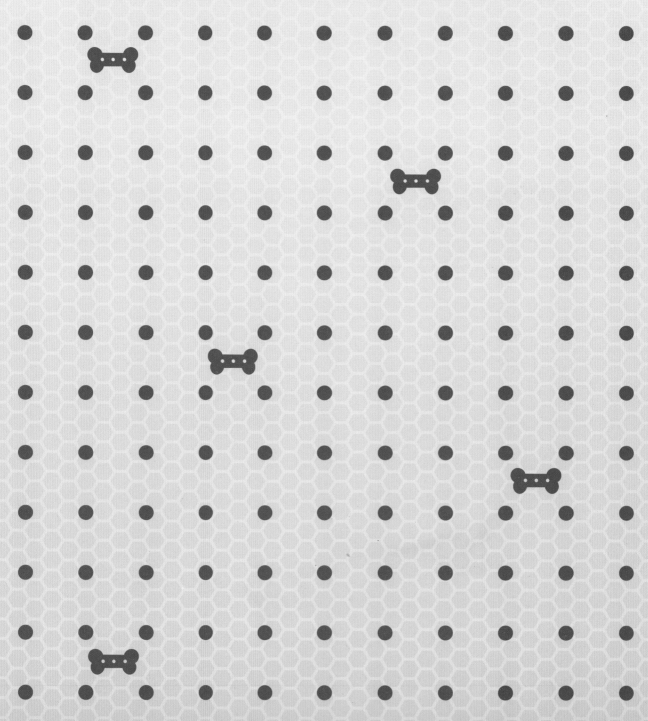

PAW PATROL

RUFF RUFF RESCUE!

PAW PATROL READY 4 ACTION!

WORK HARD PLAY HARDER

FOR YOUR PAWS ONLY!

GREAT JOB, PUPS!

Play again!

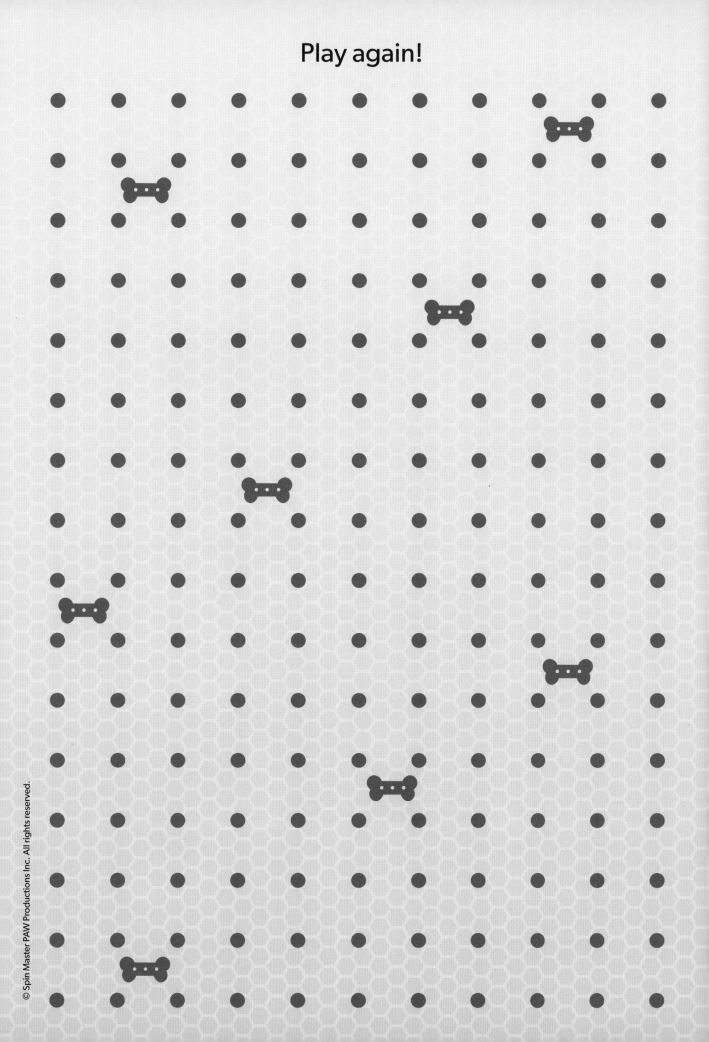

Color this picture of Marshall to match the one on the previous page.

All paws on deck!
Help Marshall and Rocky get to Ryder.

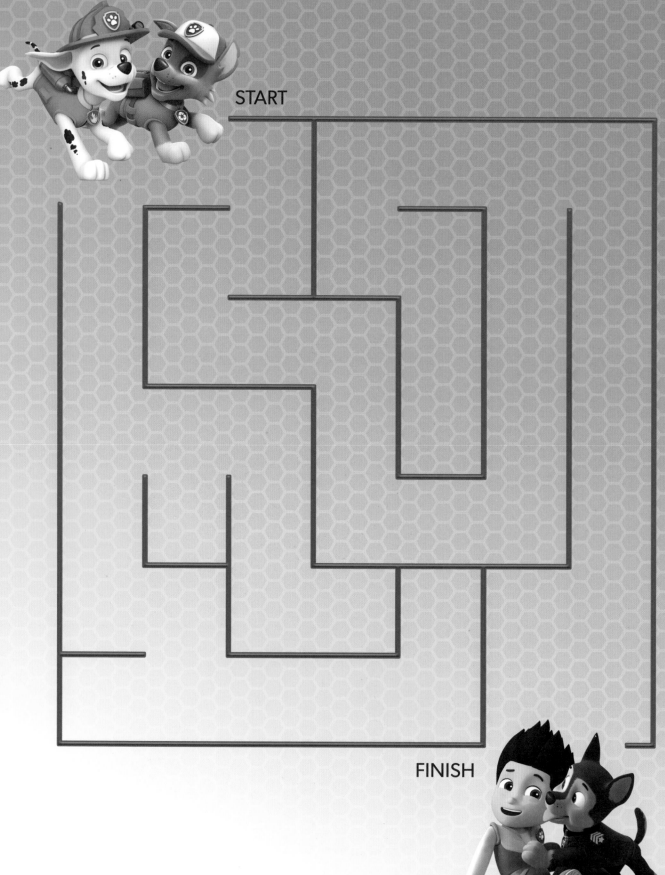

START

FINISH

Draw a helmet for Rubble.

Everest

Can you find Everest's real snowmobile?
(Hint: It's the one that's different.)

A

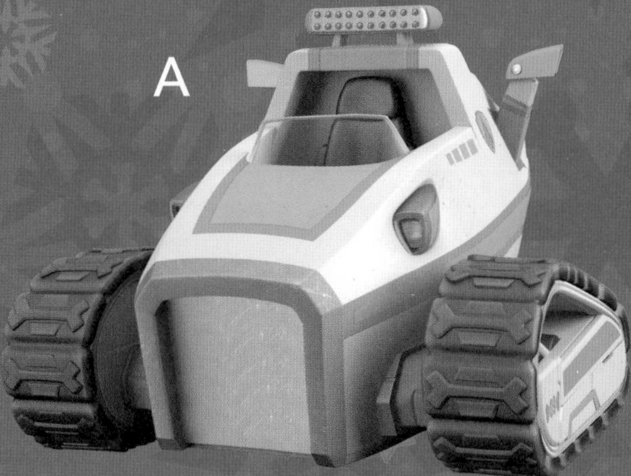

B

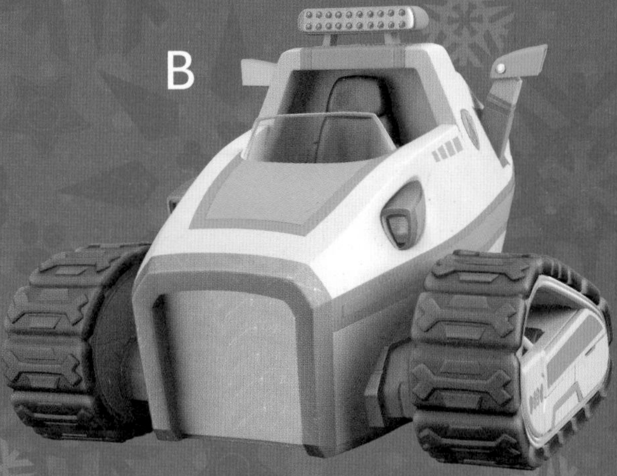

C

D

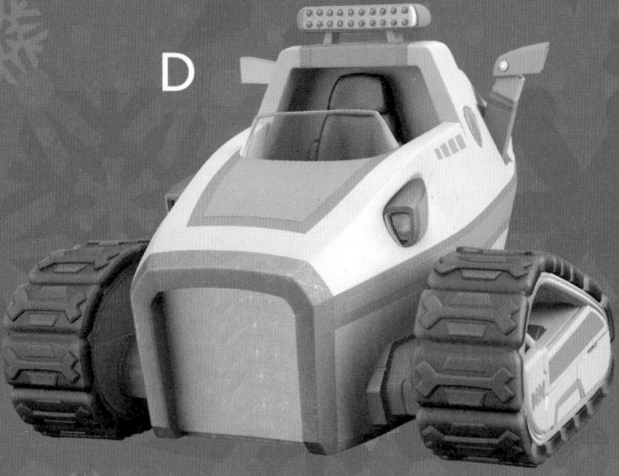

E

ANSWER: C.

The PAW Patrol is on the roll!
Use your stickers to complete the scene.

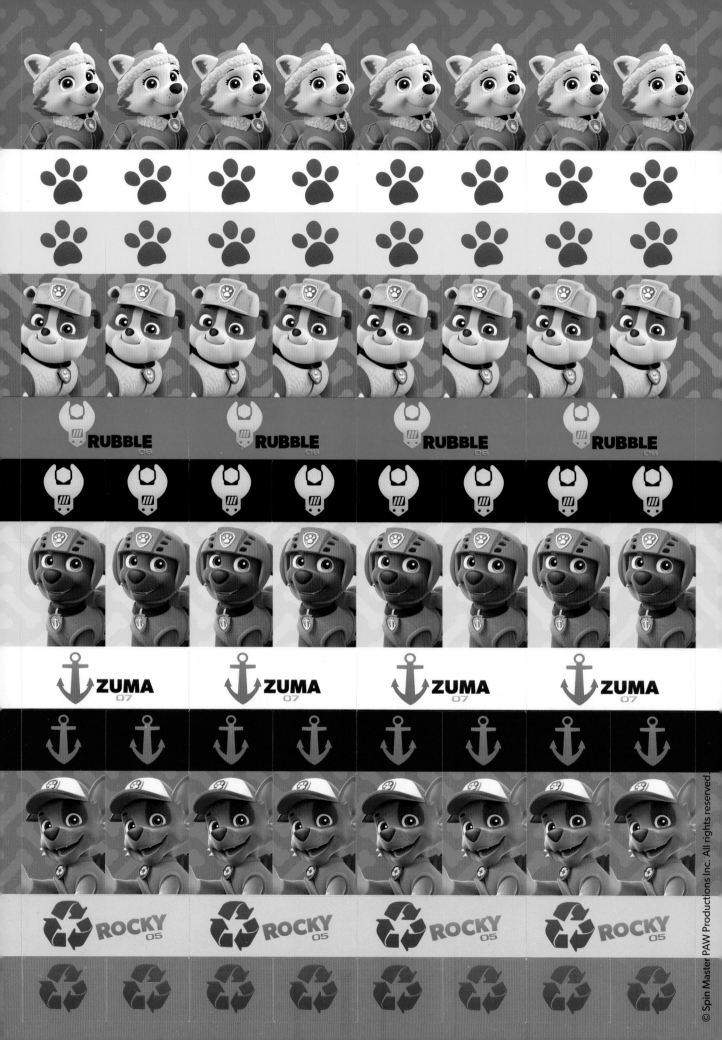

RUBBLE
06

ZUMA
07

ROCKY
05

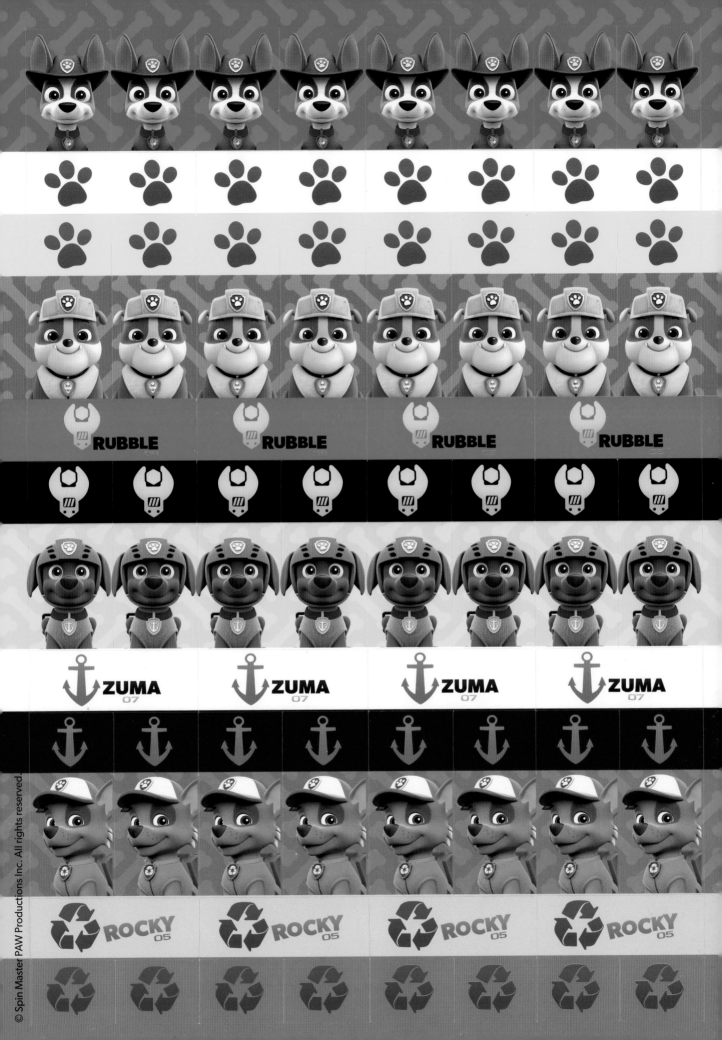

RUBBLE RUBBLE RUBBLE RUBBLE

ZUMA 07 ZUMA 07 ZUMA 07 ZUMA 07

ROCKY 05 ROCKY 05 ROCKY 05 ROCKY 05

Connect the dots to meet Rocky's new friend.

Color this picture of Skye to match the one on the previous page.

Use your stickers to match each member of the team to his or her close-up.

Draw a fish for Zuma to say hello to.

Use your stickers to match the members
of the PAW Patrol to their badges.

Use your stickers to match the members of the PAW Patrol to their badges.

Use the key to color this picture.

KEY
1 = red
2 = orange
3 = brown
4 = green
5 = yellow

Skye's got to fly!
Help her find Rubble.

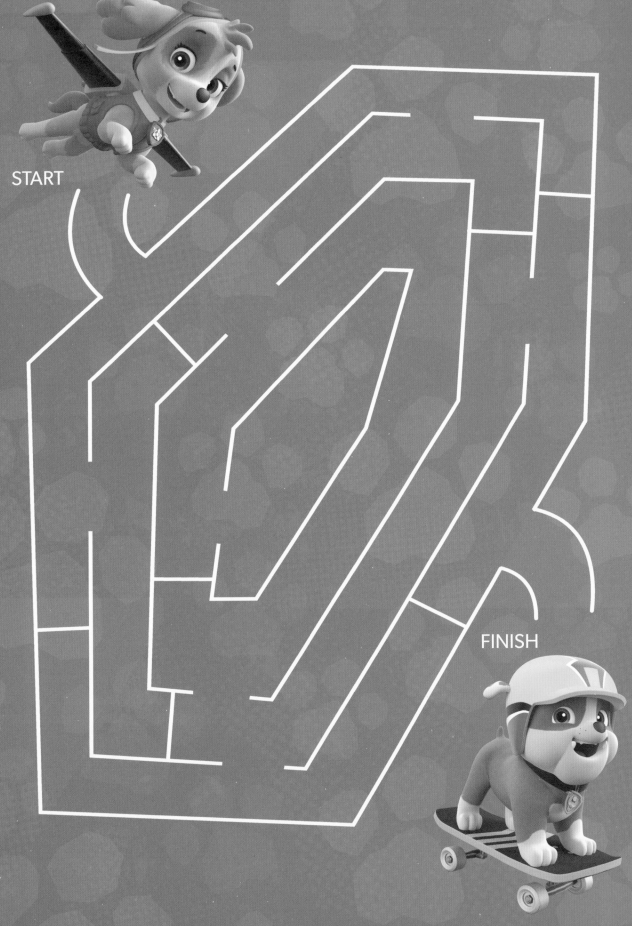

START

FINISH

TRACKER

Use the key to color this picture.

KEY

1 = gray
2 = brown
3 = green
4 = red
5 = blue

Draw a fire helmet for Marshall.

Circle the two Air Patrollers that match.

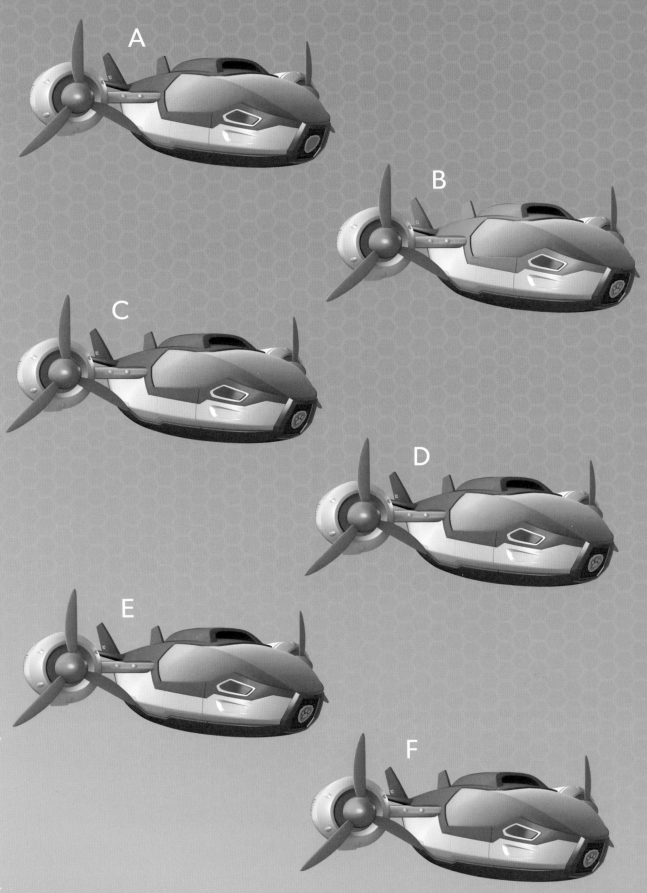

A

B

C

D

E

F

ANSWER: C and E.

Use your stickers to match each member of the team to his or her close-up.

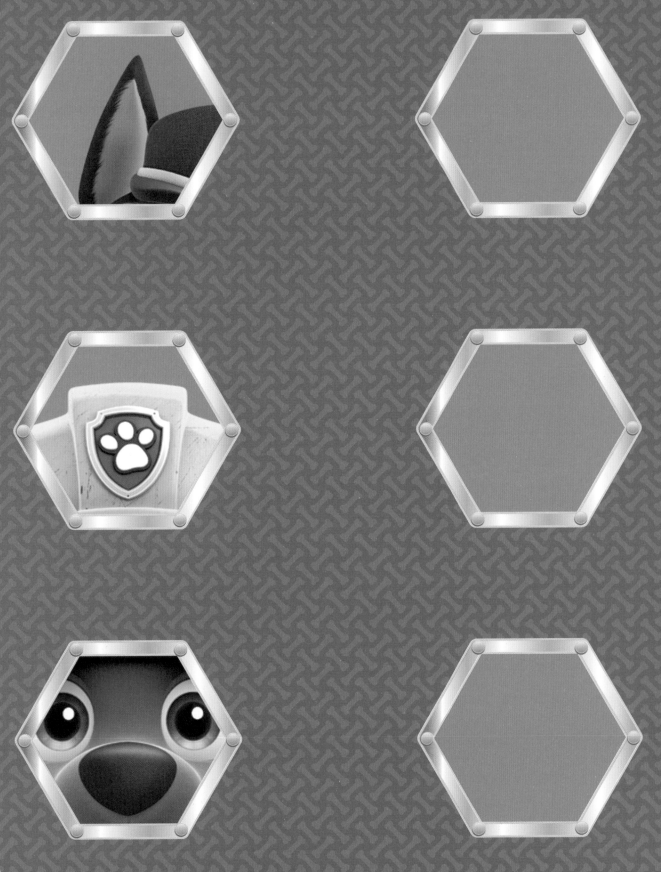

Draw a bright, shiny sun for Skye.

Use the key to color this picture.

KEY

1 = red
2 = yellow
3 = brown
4 = blue
5 = black

Chase is on the case! Help him find Rocky, but don't go past the cones.

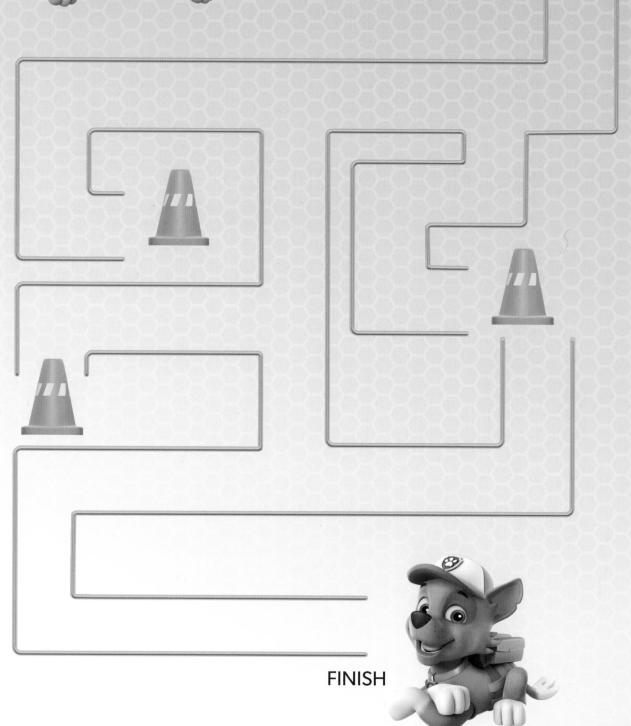

START

FINISH

Use your stickers to match each member of the team to his or her close-up.

Paw Pals!
(A game for two players)

Take turns with a friend connecting two dots with a straight line. When the line you draw completes a square, put your initials in the square and give yourself two points. If the square has a paw in it, give yourself two extra points. When all the boxes have been made, whoever has more points wins!

ROCKY

ALL PAWS on DECK!

ZUMA

MARSHALL

CHASE

BEST PUPS EVER!

RUBBLE

Play again!

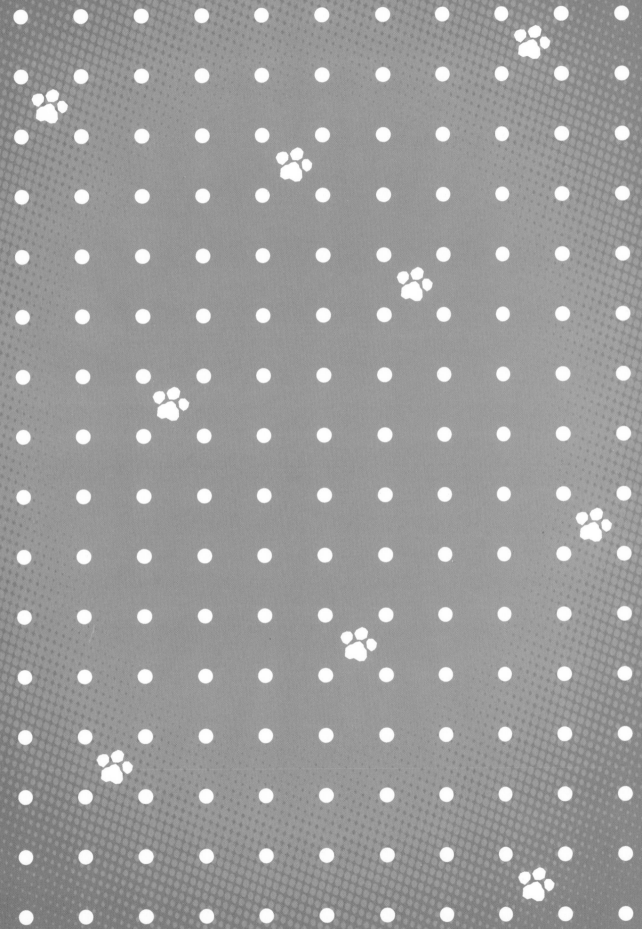

You're all good pups!
Use your stickers to complete the scene.

Draw a tasty treat for Chase.

MAKE TWO *PAW*-SOME POSTERS!

- Have a grown-up help you remove the following pages.
- Tape them together in the correct order.

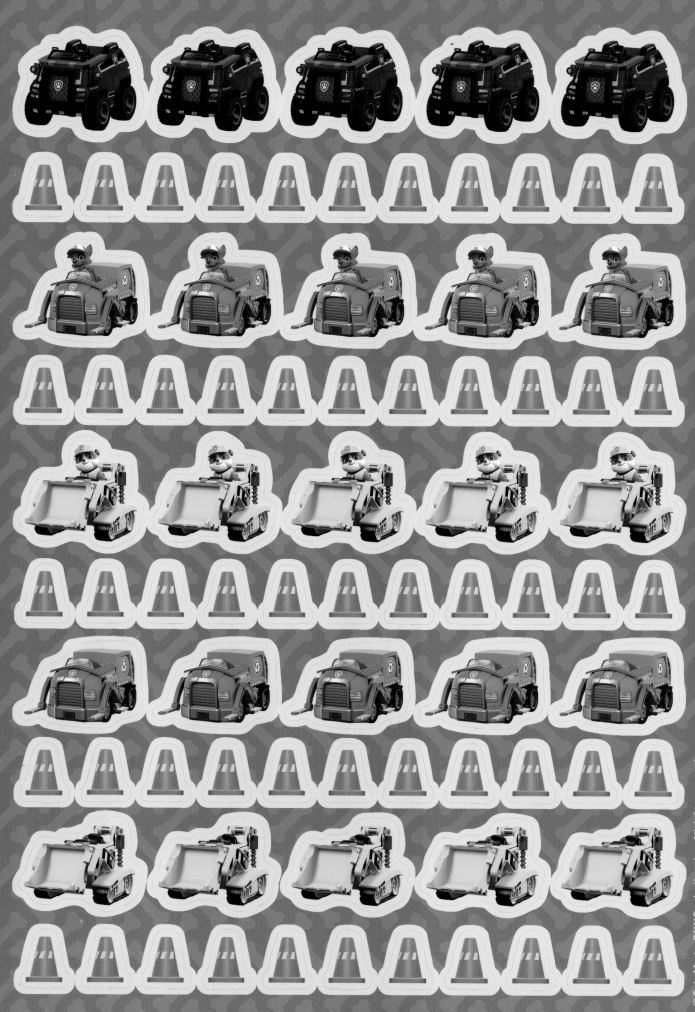

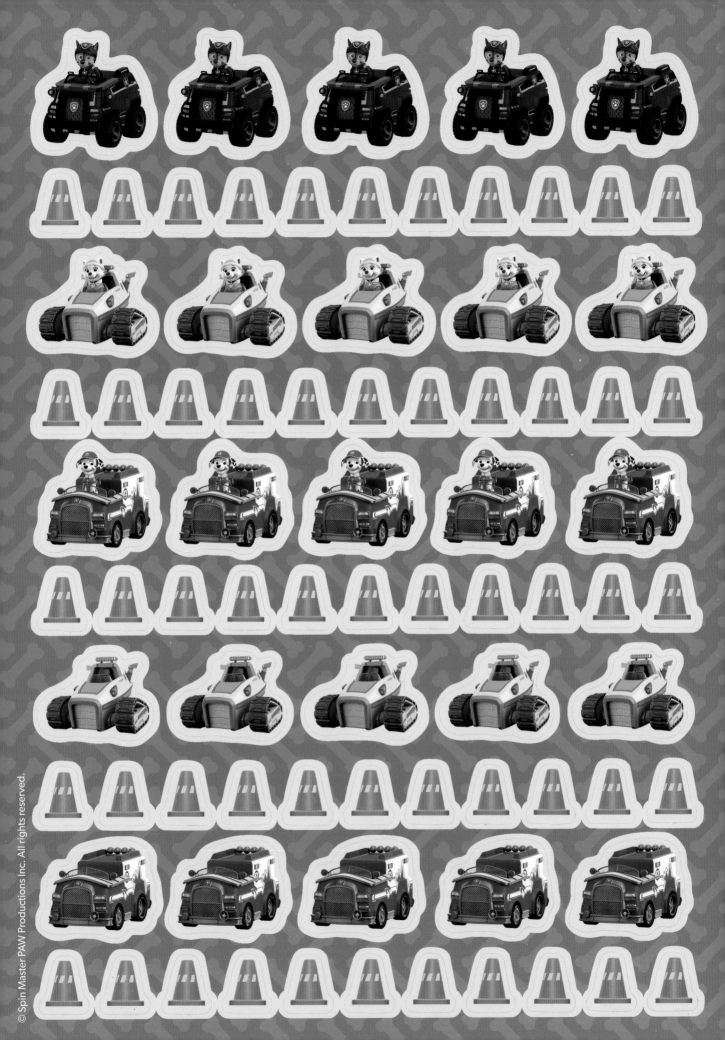

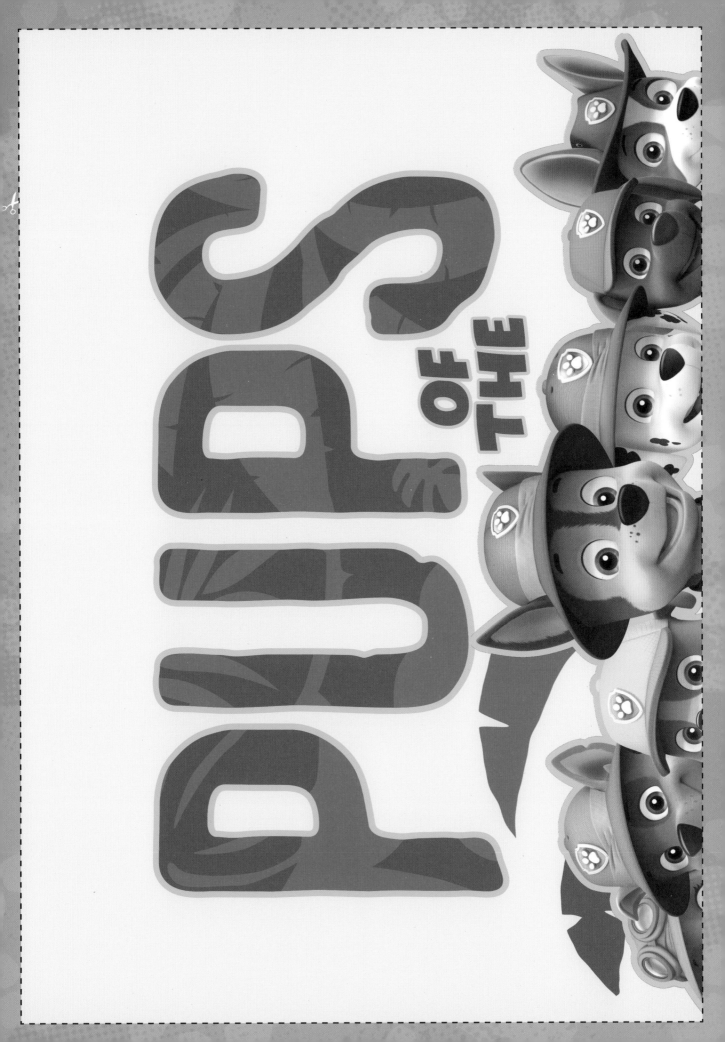